LYSTRA'S SONG

VIOLA TEMPEST

CONTENTS

IYSTRA'S SONG

VIOLA TEMPEST

CHAPTER
ONE

"GET OUT, GET OUT!"

Colton simply stood there, flabbergasted. His girl-friend of four years had just cheated on him, and yet, now *she* was the one upset, grabbing clothes from the drawers and throwing them across the room. Half of the stuff wasn't even his.

A heaping pile had collected in his arms when he said, "how could you do this, Anita?"

She turned, face flushed with red as anger burned through her entire body. "You're useless. All you do is go to that boring job you have, go home, watch television, and go to bed. You have," she counted on her fingers, "zero hobbies. You never spend time with me. We only go out once or twice a *month*. " Her chest heaved when she was done, and she raised her palms to the ceiling in a dramatic shrug. "I don't know what you expected!"

"So, you cheated on me because I'm boring?" His tone wasn't angry, but rather hurt and frustrated. He was beyond the stage of anger. That had come when he decided to surprise his girlfriend by bringing her flowers after work and found another man in her bed. It had escalated when she didn't even deny it, telling him she hadn't been trying to hide it. Now he was simply defeated. "Did our relationship mean nothing to you?"

"I cheated on you." She inhaled deeply, closing her eyes to compose herself. She wanted it to be over, but she didn't want to turn the conversation into something it didn't have to be. "I cheated on you because I need something different, Colton. I need someone who will actually pay attention."

"I see," he said, shifting his weight to grab a pair of his pants up off the floor.

"Even now!" she screamed, temper rising once again. "You're simply admitting defeat. You're so useless that you don't even fight for your own girlfriend!"

Colton didn't say anything. The thing was, he was too stunned to speak. He wanted to beg, wanted to plead with her to stay. He wanted to tell her to get rid of the other man and stay with him because he'd change for her. In his mind, he loved her completely and honestly. But he couldn't bring his mouth to move and form the words.

"Get out of my house," she hissed, throwing a pair of his shoes atop the pile in his arms.

He turned and left the bedroom. He thought that maybe he would come back later when she'd calmed down and become more rational. When she realized that she needed him and his secure office job to continue paying off her mortgage.

A young, blonde-haired man sat in the living room without his shirt, one leg crossed over the other. "Bad luck, man," he said, reaching his hand into a bag of Colton's chips, pulling one out and popping it into his mouth. "She's quite the catch. You guys done?"

"Yeah," Colton said absentmindedly. He was still focused on the fact that this man was sitting on the couch that *he* had purchased, that *he* had sat on so many times. Anita had chosen this man over him, and that fact stung.

"Look, I didn't know she had a man. I mean, I *knew* since your clothes are here, but we're just casual. Thought you knew."

Colton stared at this man, not taking in much of what he said, and left without another word. His car was still in the driveway, so he threw everything into the back seat and climbed into the front. He sat there for a while, gripping the steering wheel and resting his forehead against his knuckles. No tears slipped from his eyes yet, but they threatened to with every exhale.

He continued to sit there until Anita came running out of the house. She burst through the front door, screaming incoherently and shooing him with her hands until he turned on the car and backed it out of the driveway.

Colton drove for a while, no aim or direction in his mind. He simply drove, turning when the road ended or when he felt the urge to. He wasn't even sure where he was anymore. The roads and buildings had started to become unfamiliar long ago.

He wouldn't have stopped driving at all if it weren't for the fact that his gas gauge was soon down to nearly zero.

He pulled into a gas station, still on the edge of

breaking. Barely registering anything around him, he felt numb. While he pumped the gas, he couldn't hear the traffic or the people or the person a lane over asking him what to do if the button won't work. In fact, he didn't notice anything at all until he went inside, paid, and was on his way back out to his car.

There was an antique store across the street, one he hadn't noticed while pulling into the station. He felt drawn to go inside and look around. Perhaps he'd find something old to spend his money on that he could destroy and feel good about himself again. He'd never had destructive tendencies before, but something about how he felt was drawing him toward that outlet.

Colton got back into his car, but only for a moment until he crossed the empty street and made his way into the plaza's parking lot. He knew his small red Toyota wouldn't be able to handle a table or anything large, but perhaps a vase, a chair, or even a very large picture frame. His palms became sweaty. He'd never been so impulsive before, and it felt good to walk into a store with no idea what he would come out with. Was this what Anita meant when she'd told him she needed something different?

He could be different. He *would* be different, for her.

He entered the store, the bell ringing loudly overhead. Inside, furniture lined the walls. Aisles were created out of chairs, tables, and other pieces of furniture that looked decades or centuries old. There were some bare spots — though not many — that indicated where a piece had been recently moved or bought.

"Can I help you with anything?" A man's voice asked, clear as the bell from before. He wore a blue plaid shirt and jeans, his long white beard coming down just past his collarbone. His eyes were wide and kind, staring at Colton with a wide, toothy smile.

"Uh, no. Just browsing," Colton replied, hardly recognizing the scratchy, near-incoherent voice that came out. The old man seemed to have understood, because he nodded and returned to reading the newspaper before him.

Colton wandered around for a while, but nothing immediately caught his eye. He saw the sentimental value in everything. He couldn't break hundred-year-old China that had been hand-crafted. He couldn't stand the thought of even touching the wooden children's toys.

He was about to give up and go home, thinking he might stop at a thrift store instead. But then, his eyes caught something. Something beautiful that he could never think to destroy. Something to give him purpose. A piano. A hobby.

He walked over to the large, solid black grand piano. It looked — unlike the rest of the store — like nobody had bothered to dust it in months. Cobwebs hung off it in thick strings. He touched his finger to one of the notes, and it rang out in tune.

"The old owners took great care of it. Never played it, though." Colton jumped. He hadn't heard the owner walk up behind him.

His heart beating out of his chest, he managed to ask, "how come?"

"Lady said it was haunted. Honestly? I believe her." The man went to reach out a finger to touch the wood, but thought better of it and retracted his hand. "I can hear it playing sometimes when the store is empty."

"Maybe it's not empty, then?" He never was a skeptic, and Colton knew when, sometimes, the most obvious answer was the right one. "Kids have their own version of fun."

"Look," the store owner said, backing up a few too-casual steps. "Take it if you want. But don't say I didn't warn you."

"How much?" Colton asked without hesitation. If this shop owner was so ready to be rid of it, perhaps he could get a pretty good deal.

"You got a truck?" he asked, shoving wrinkled hands into the pockets of his jeans.

Colton shook his head. "Just my hatchback."

"I'll charge you for delivery only. My son can be

here in fifteen minutes, tops. He'll load it into his pickup and follow behind to your house. Fair?"

Colton nodded, and the man stated his price. It was laughably cheap, not nearly enough what it was worth. The piano had to be a hundred and fifty years old just by looking at the structure of it. If he had been in his right state of mind, he might have been thrown off by the ridiculous price the owner had set. He might have thought twice before purchasing something thought to be haunted.

After paying at the counter, Colton waited patiently for the owner's son to arrive. Internally, the store owner was celebrating the sale of this piano after three years of it sitting in his store, collecting dust. If he had known it would cause this much trouble, he wouldn't have bothered purchasing it from that panicked lady in the first place.

Colton walked over to the piano and sat at the bench that came with the piece. He ran his hands along the keys, taking a deep breath into his lungs. He touched the same key as before, and then hit another, lower note. His fingers splayed over the keys, waiting for his instruction.

"You play?" A younger male voice asked.

Colton turned around to see who he assumed to be the owner's son, standing there with one of his friends right next to him.

"Oh, not really," Colton said, standing up and wiping his sweaty palms on his pants. "I played a bit as a kid, but nothing really stuck."

"Well, good luck," the kid said, and he and his friend stepped forward to pick up the piano. "I've heard it playing at night. It's something freaky; I'll tell you that much."

The two of them managed to maneuver the piano onto the back of the pickup with little difficulty. Colton felt once again useless as he stood there, watching but of no help at all. Anita's hateful words flooded back to him, but he shook them from his head. He would show her that he had talent, that he wasn't useless in the slightest. Who knew if he had some sort of hidden aptitude for it now that he was older, mature, and disciplined?

Colton led the men to his house, where he was determined to figure out a way to get *his* Anita back.

CHAPTER

TWO

As much as he had previously been excited about his new piano-playing prospect, Colton hadn't touched the keys once since the antique shop owner's son dropped it off, set everything up, and left. Perhaps the instrument would just be a decoration. He could call Anita over and tell her that he was trying, or even fake the talent altogether.

He sat at the dining table all by himself — not having bothered to turn on any lights — sipping on the melatonin tea Anita had once gotten him as a gift. He didn't like the taste, but it made him fall asleep, and he was sure he'd need the help tonight. It was nearly midnight, and he still felt wide awake.

The total darkness was only ever momentarily disturbed by flashes of lightning. This was closely followed by loud crashes of thunder that rattled the frames on his walls. It didn't faze him; in fact, he felt numb to it all. It wasn't worth the effort to try to be amazed, scared, or even interested in the weather outside.

His mind was so, so tired, and yet his eyes refused to close, even with the help of the tea. He took another sip, attempting to will his body into compliance. A picture frame across the room caught his attention, and he set the mug down on the table with a bit more force than he'd intended to. He stood and stalked over to the wall, glancing at the photo with a newfound rage.

The image captured a moment from one of his and Anita's first dates. They'd gone to the beach for a stroll and a picnic, and the memory of the day was one he'd cherish forever. In the photo, the ocean was illumi-nated in orange from the setting sun behind them. She was holding onto him from behind, her arms around his neck, and legs around his waist. She was planting a kiss on his cheek, and his smile was broader than it ever had been before. He wasn't even sure he'd smiled like that since.

He grabbed the frame off the wall and threw it. It shattered against the wall, and glass spewed in every direction. His chest heaved, teeth grinding so hard that he thought they might file down to nothing.

When the hairs on his neck stood on end, his anger dissolved nearly immediately. He didn't feel alone all of a sudden. But when he spun around, looking for someone, there was nobody there. The feeling vanished entirely.

Colton shivered. Perhaps he *was* tired, after all. He picked up the half-empty mug and tossed it into the sink haphazardly. He didn't bother rinsing it out or throwing it into the dishwasher, something he knew he would regret the next morning.

He trudged his way up the stairs, and when he made it to his bedroom, he didn't even bother stripping himself from his clothes before pulling down the covers and slipping under them. His room was bland, he knew, and Anita had always complained about the lack of decoration. Perhaps, she'd had a point in saying that he was useless and boring.

Colton twisted around, facing the spot where Anita used to lie. He reached out a hand, his fingers reaching for the cold space. If he squinted just enough, he could almost see her sleeping figure next to him. He could almost pretend that everything was okay, and he wasn't utterly and completely alone.

A SWEET MELODY FILLED THE AIR, THE CRESCENDO OF music reaching higher and higher. A woman's hands flew over the keys with perfect grace, not missing a single note. Her hands moved faster and faster until they were nothing but flesh-toned blurs.

Just as the notes hit their peak, the woman's fingers slipped, and it made a horrible, crashing noise. She cringed and smiled up at the man, who was standing on the other side of the grand, wooden piano. They both wore nineteenth-century clothing and seemed perfectly content in them.

"Sorry dear," the woman said. "I just can't get that last part right."

The man smiled. He always smiled. "No worries. You'll get it one day."

"Promise?" the woman asked. They'd had this conversation many times now, and it always went the same.

The man walked around and kissed the woman on the top of her head. "I promise," he said. He looked up at the sheet before her. "Perhaps if you take out a few notes—"

"No," the woman said, grabbing the sheets of music and folding them down. "I won't hear it. It's my song, and that's how I want it to be played."

As if he'd expected that answer, the man said, "of course, darling."

EVERYTHING WENT DARK. THE TERRIBLE SOUND OF something snapping, and a high-pitched woman's screams, filled the air. Pain, horrible pain. Endless suffering followed, along with sorrow that could never be healed.

Loss. That's what that feeling was: loss.

Flashes of agony, and then nothing. But nothing was just as unsettling as feeling everything at once. Floating with no ground... no body, no soul, no Earth, no anything at all.

No, no, no, no.

And then, there was a thread. A singular thread of pain that could be grasped and held onto. Everything came back, just as powerful and painful as before. But this time, that something was a breath of fresh air. More than anything, there was opportunity.

Even if the walls felt like they were caving in.

A GRAVE WAS NEXT. HALF-BURIED IN SNOW AND aged with time. The name was no longer comprehensible. No flowers had adorned this grave for years, as it was long forgotten within a sea of others. Somewhere else, a woman sobbed. But not here, not under this large, dying tree in the back of a place nobody would remember.

A crow cawed, landing atop the gravestone and pecking at the moss that had accumulated in the cracks. It would make a fine nest for something new.

MUSIC AGAIN. THIS TIME, THERE WAS NOTHING BUT the darkness consuming all and everything. It sounded as if there were three pianists all playing slightly different harmonies, but it was just simply the one. Ten fingers, two hands, and one woman.

No lyrics, as lyrics were not needed to convey the emotion of the piece. Simply the emotions of one woman, keeping herself tethered to this Earth through the music her fingers remembered how to play.

Always the same woman. Always the same song. Never the same audience.

Colton's eyes flew open as a crash of thunder filled the room. He sat up in his bed and rubbed his face. *What an odd, senseless dream.* A cold sweat clung to his body, dampening his clothes in uncomfortable areas.

Then, as the sound of thunder faded out and reduced to silence, he heard music. The same music as in his dream, as if it had never stopped. His heart jumped in his chest, fear suddenly welling up inside him. Had someone broken in?

Cursing himself for not owning some sort of bat or weapon, he swung his legs off the bed and stood. His limbs were stiff and sore, as if he'd slept for days without moving. He walked across the carpet to the door, trying to keep as silent as possible.

He twisted the knob, and his door swung open, creaking at the hinges. Still, the music didn't stop playing.

Luckily, the carpeted floor allowed for silent movement down the hallway and toward the stairs. The music grew louder with every step, but he wasn't sure if it was just because of his increasing proximity. Whoever it was, seemed to be pressing their fingers more angrily against the keys, taking a more aggressive approach to the beautiful song.

At last, when he reached the bottom of the stairs and only had one wall separating him from the intruder, he took a deep breath. He reminded himself that he was strong, that he was a fighter. Whoever it was simply played the piano, and although they played it well, he would be catching them completely off-guard.

As he completed his personal pep talk in his head, he peered around the corner, testing to see who the intruder might be.

The ghostly-white, translucent figure of a woman sat upon the bench, head bobbing slightly with the beat of the music. He couldn't tell, but it seemed like the same girl from his dream. Her long, flowing hair came halfway down her back. She wore a dark green and gold revealing dress, made from the thinnest material, and looked young — about his age.

He stepped into the room, and the girl's head spun around to face him. He went still, but she gasped and winked out of existence so suddenly that he didn't know if she'd been there at all.

After letting his heart rate calm, Colton walked cautiously over to the piano. He waved his hands in front of him, checking the air for... something. When nothing revealed itself as being amiss, Colton sat down on the bench where the woman had been only moments before.

His hands found their way to the keys. He knew he wouldn't be able to play anything close to what he had heard, but his fingers found a mind of their own. They flew, playing the scales he'd thought he had long forgotten. He smiled to himself, leaning back and closing his eyes. A cold wave passed through his entire body, and he smiled. At least he was feeling *something*.

And at last, Colton Brodie thought he found something worth wasting time for.

The broken man paced around the living room for days on end. It wouldn't stop, the pacing, the muttering. He'd leave for a few hours during the day, and at night, he would sit down at her piano and fumble his hands along her keys. He'd sleep, but always either on the couch or passed out at the piano.

Lystra began to feel sorry for the man. He'd obviously suffered some sort of tragedy in his life and, well, she wasn't a stranger to tragedy.

The amount of coffee this man would drink was insurmountable. And she knew very well why. The dreams and nightmares would be unbearable by now, and the moment he figured out that it was the piano creating the fuss, she'd likely be back at that antique shop to be bought by another. There was always another.

Colton was the broken man's name, though she didn't know it yet. But she did know that he wasn't the man she was looking for, not nearly. The man she was looking for was long dead, stolen by time.

So, she tried to keep to herself, for the most part. She loved playing, but she knew that any more instances would draw his attention and might drive him further into madness. She had enough humanity left in her to know that she didn't want to cause his mind to break completely. That would simply be cruel; and although she was many things, she never considered herself to be wicked.

DAYS PASSED, AND HE GREW WORSE AND WORSE. He didn't shave and barely even showered. She was almost certain that the same clothes he wore everyday would smell atrocious by now. They certainly looked wrinkled and unwashed. His house was in the same state, with discarded cups everywhere and a distinct lack of motivation to clean up after himself.

This cycle continued, until one night, when Colton sat at the piano, hands hovering over the keys. He waited for something, anything to happen. Perhaps the same reverie that had occurred that first night he'd brought the instrument home. He waited for a few moments, but nothing happened. He stood abruptly, knocking the stool over behind him and shouting out in anger and frustration.

He went over to where Anita's broken picture was still laying on the ground and stepped on it again, feeling the satisfying crunch under his slipper-clad foot. He reached down and, being somewhat mindful of the glass, pulled out the photo. He tore the picture to shreds and threw it up like confetti.

But the itch hadn't been scratched. He walked around the room to where a vase filled with wilted flowers sat on a table. He picked it up and threw it across the room, where it shattered against the wall. Smiling, he grabbed a discarded, three-day-old mug and hurled it in the same direction. Coffee and shards of China sprayed everywhere, ruining the carpet. But when he lifted his diploma off the wall, Lystra decided it was time to step in.

"You really shouldn't destroy your—"

Colton screamed, dropping the diploma onto the ground. It cracked, but didn't explode like all the others.

"You can see me?" Lystra asked, cocking her head to the side. This had never happened before. Usually, it was just the piano-playing that alerted her presence, or sometimes, her voice if the living person was in enough distress.

"What the hell? Are you a *ghost*?"

She looked down at herself. She floated in the air a half inch above the ground, and her translucent figure depicted the same young woman wearing the same dress that he had glimpsed days ago. "It appears that way."

She floated around him, getting a good look for the first time. "I'm Lystra, by the way."

"Colton," the broken man gasped out. His mouth was hanging open, and his eyes tracked her every movement. So, he *could* see her. "Am I crazy?"

She crossed her arms across her chest. "How should I know that?"

He reached out a hand, and it went right through her upper abdomen. She yelped and fell backwards through the air, hissing out a curse as she did.

"Sorry," Colton said, bringing his hand back and

caressing it. The moment he had touched her, the whole limb had gone terribly cold.

"You *dare* disrespect me like that?" Her beautiful face turned livid. "I'd have half a thought to *make* you go crazy."

"No, I—I'm sorry," Colton stuttered out. A ghost, a ghost, a ghost, a ghost. A ghost was in his living room.

"Why did you buy my piano, anyway?" she asked, all previous anger gone. She floated over to the bench, where she glared at the fallen stool. "Do you mind?"

He rushed forward and righted it for her. She sat down, her dress elegantly falling so it looked like she was sitting. Her posture was perfect, as it always was. She'd always prided herself on her exquisite structure.

She pretended to crack her knuckles, but it made no sound. When she placed her fingers upon the keys, the piano began to play. It was the same tune as the first night, but this time, she started from the beginning. A shiver traveled up Colton's spine as the music spun a sad, sorrowful tale.

"Where did you learn to play?" he asked, and the music paused abruptly.

She turned to glare at him. "Why do you ask so many questions?"

He didn't have an answer for that. Instead, he decided to reply to her earlier inquiry. "I bought the piano because, well... I thought I might learn how to play."

"By yourself, without a teacher? You'd be better off getting a set of bongos." Her hands floated over the keys, pretending to play but not actually hitting the keys. Her fingers remembered every note, every sound without actually making it.

He shrugged. "My girlfriend said I should get a hobby."

"Ah," she said, though she wasn't interested at all. Her nose wrinkled slightly, and she shook out her hands before restarting the motions.

"Ex-girlfriend," he clarified. "I should probably start calling her my ex."

"So, this woman broke up with you because you couldn't play the piano? And now you've bought a piano that you don't know how to play." She chuckled, though her entire focus was still on her hands. "Very smart, Colton."

He coughed, averting his eyes. Suddenly, his house looked like an absolute mess. Shattered glass over the floor, old cups of coffee dotting the dining and living rooms. Dishes were piled high in the sink, and he couldn't remember the last time he'd cleaned.

Lystra didn't notice while Colton had this realization. She simply sat questioningly before her instrument, a dazed look on her face and no thoughts in her mind except following the music.

"She was everything to me, but I caught her in bed with another man. So, I bought the piano to prove her wrong — prove myself wrong, I guess."

"You want to play to prove to yourself that you deserve her." It wasn't a question, but Colton still nodded. "And you still want her even though she cheated on you."

"Well, when you put it that way—"

"What way should I put it then, Colton?" Her tone was exasperated. Honestly, she didn't care for those types of mortal squabbles. She'd seen enough at this point that it all seemed pointless. From her perspective, everything was simple. There was pain, and then there wasn't. Chase what eased the pain, and run from what caused it. Many things could be avoided this way.

He didn't have an answer for her. They were silent for a while, Colton toeing at the carpet with his slippers. He thought back on his relationship with Anita. Everything good in his life had come from her, everything fun. But now, he could have something of his own.

"Do you think *you* could teach me?" Colton asked finally.

Lystra whipped her head around, staring at him as

if she'd forgotten he was there. The look faded, and became contemplative. "Perhaps."

"Perhaps?" Colton asked, still standing in the middle of the room. "What would you like in return? I could... pay you?"

She laughed, the sound echoing throughout the house. "I'm dead, fool. I have no need for money."

"Then what?" he asked, growing more irritated. "What can I offer you?"

She swiveled toward him on the stool. She crossed one leg over the other and said, "You can get my song out there. Show it to the world, and let everyone know that I, Lystra Flowers, created this masterpiece."

"Done," he said without thinking. In reality, he had no idea how to put a song out into the world. But he could try, right? An honest attempt was better than nothing.

"And," she said, raising a finger, "I want you to leave the television on while you're not home."

He opened his mouth, but then cocked his head to the side. "The television?"

"It's dreadfully lonely existing within a piano with hardly any way to entertain myself. Besides, it wasn't around yet when I was still alive, so it fascinates me. Leave it on, any channel will do, and I'll teach you how to play."

He nodded. "I can do that."

He hadn't known that ghosts even existed, let alone that they could get bored. He supposed it made sense, in a way.

"When can we start?" he asked, making for the bench.

"After you clean up this place." He stopped in his tracks and turned to face her. "You've made a mess everywhere, and I can't stand to perform in it. Blasphemous."

With that, she vanished from existence. No rebuttals, then.

He made quick work of the house, using gloves to put the large chunks of glass into reinforced garbage bags and vacuuming the rest. He used a stain remover to lift up most of the coffee stains, and was able to run a few loads in the dishwasher. Afterwards, it looked just like it always had: perfectly unoriginal.

"Alright," he said into the air when he was done, but nobody answered. "I'm done now; when can we start?"

Nothing happened. No ghostly woman figure appeared; the piano didn't even sound a single note.

He thought that maybe he was tired; maybe he had dreamt the whole thing. But it had felt so real, so *right* that he dismissed that idea. She was just resting, he supposed. She'd be back tomorrow night.

Lystra waited until the dead of night, when Colton

was fast asleep upstairs, before she played her tune again. And this time, her hands didn't falter once. A smile stretched across her face. Indeed, it was time to share her creation with the world.

FOUR

"You really *DO* suck." Lystra observed, lounging atop the piano with her face in her hands. "I don't know how you've gone through life being this bad at the piano."

Colton's face flushed. "Not everyone can be a genius like you," he said, gritting his teeth and grinding them hard against each other.

Lystra laughed. "I'm glad you think that, but no. Anyone can play if they put enough effort into it. Here, watch my fingers."

She floated down to sit next to him on the bench. His entire left side chilled, but he was getting used to the feeling. She laid her hands across the keys, took a deep breath, and played four notes.

Colton mimicked the first three flawlessly, but he hit the wrong note on the fourth, cringing at the dull sound. He shoved his hands under his armpits. "It's useless."

"Put your hands back up," she snapped, and he did so. She laid her hands atop his, but he barely felt the cold. "You hit the index here, then two beats with the middle finger. Don't hit the last note with your ring finger; use your pinky. Like this." Her hands shifted, and he followed. The resulting note rang out true and clear. She pulled her hands away and looked at him expectantly.

He did exactly as she told him to, and the notes were the same. A huge grin spread across his face. "I did it!"

"Try again, but faster," she said, though she smiled.

His hands tried again and again, slightly increasing the pace each time. When his confidence grew, he tried going at the same speed as Lystra, but his hands slipped over the keys. He grumbled in frustration, but made one more attempt. When it failed, he threw his hands into the air.

"It's useless," he said, shaking his head.

"If you can get this part, I'll answer one question that you have." She crossed her arms over her chest, daring him to try again.

He thought about it for a moment. "You're on."

It took him a total of five more tries to get the section right. When he did, he stood and cheered, pumping his fist into the air with primal elation. In a moment of excitement, he went to hug Lystra. When his arms went right through her body, he stepped back, a sheepish expression finding its way across his face. "Sorry."

She dusted off her shoulders as if his hands had wrinkled her dress. "Ask your question, Colton." Her tone was light, only slightly disapproving.

"What's it like being a ghost?"

She didn't answer for a few heartbeats. He was about to apologize again when she said, "you're the first person to be able to see me. Do you know how lonely it is to be trapped inside a piano, unable to speak to or interact with anyone? When I *do* try communicating, people are afraid. Terrified. One man even tried smashing my piano to bits, but realized he could probably get some money off this antique piano if he marketed it correctly."

Colton just nodded. He had no words for what she was going through, what she had endured. He wished — perhaps foolishly — that she never had to experience it at all.

"People are greedy and selfish. I've come to understand that now more than ever." She shook her head, absent-mindedly running her hands over the fabric covering her lap.

"Not everyone," he said. "You just have to find the right people."

She cocked her head to the side. "Are *you* the right people, Colton?"

He wanted to tell her that yes, he was indeed a selfless and caring individual. But he couldn't lie, not to her. "I'm still trying to figure that out."

Satisfied with that answer, she patted the spot next to herself. He sat back down, adjusting a few times until he could comfortably rest his foot back onto the pedal.

"How *did* you die?" Colton blurted out before he could stop the words from forming.

"I suggest you don't repeat that question," she said without hesitation. Her face and tone had gone deadly calm. "It isn't polite."

"Sorry, I'm not exactly up-to-date on my ghost etiquette. I'm a bit rusty."

"Now is not the time for jokes. Now, I want you to

do the next four notes." He opened his mouth, but she held up a hand. "If the question isn't about piano, it will wait until *after* you've mastered the notes."

"How did you know I was about to ask a question? I could have been about to say 'you're the most wonderful instructor, Lystra.' But now... I guess you'll never know."

She glared. "Were you?"

"Well, no. But—"

"Colton!"

"Alright, alright," he said, setting his hands onto the cold keys.

She showed him the next part of the song a total of three times, going slower each time so he could memorize where exactly to put his hands.

It took about fifteen minutes of scolding and bickering between them for him to finally wrap his brain around the set. In the end, it actually wasn't that hard. He just didn't know piano very well.

"Put them both together," she said, sitting back and jerking her chin toward the keys.

Not allowing himself to second guess, he flew through the first four notes and launched into the next. There were a few moments where he hesitated on the next note, but generally, it could be passable as a song's introduction.

He laughed and played it again. But this time,

when he finished those eight notes, Lystra continued on. She picked up where he left off; her left hand played the chords and pressed down as her right flew. A shiver shot down his spine, and he watched with a newfound appreciation for her talent.

By the end, she was smiling. "I almost feel alive again when I play."

"Is this the only song you know?" When she grinned at him, he realized that he had just unintentionally spent his question. It would have likely been something similar to that anyway, so he wasn't too disappointed.

"No, but it's my favorite. I wrote it myself." She thought for a moment, and started into a different song. A sad, slow song; it was a lullaby of sorts. It didn't have the same rise and fall as the other song, but rather, spun a darker tune.

"Why can't you teach me that one?" he asked, watching her hands as they graced over the black and white keys, touching them with such love. "It looks easier."

"Because that's not the deal. I teach you *my* song, and you share it with the world. Besides, this one is much too sensitive for you. The way you play... you'd ruin the entire meaning."

His eyes narrowed. "Is it because I'm a guy?"

"A hot-headed, egotistical, and impatient man who is incapable of the emotion required for this song."

"I think you underestimate how tender I can be," he said, his voice lowering deep into his chest.

For the first time in a while, she was speechless. If she had a circulatory system, she was sure that her heart would be pounding and her face flushed. Not knowing what to do, she looked toward the window on the other side of the room.

"It's getting late, and don't you have work tomorrow? We can continue tomorrow afternoon," she said, and vanished without another word.

She watched as he stood from the bench, stretched his stiff limbs, and walked up the stairs toward his bedroom.

For the first time in a very long time, she was experiencing the emotions that truly mattered.

COLTON PACED AROUND HIS ROOM, HIS PHONE clutched tightly in his hand. A number was already typed into the number pad, but his dilemma laid in whether or not he wanted to call.

"No," he said aloud to himself. "I won't. I can't, and I won't."

His thumb went to exit the calling app, but instead,

he hit the dial icon. His mouth fell open, his entire body freezing. He heard his phone ringing once, twice, and he didn't know what to do.

"Hello?" a groggy voice asked on the other end. "Who is it?"

He brought the phone to his ear, but couldn't say anything.

"Who's calling you this late?" a male's voice asked distantly.

Colton knew that voice, but pretended he hadn't heard it. It was easier that way.

"Probably a scammer," the female's voice responded.

"Hey, Anita," Colton said softly. "I just wanted—"

"Oh. You." Her annoyed tone was what he'd expected, but not what he had hoped. She sighed. "Look, you've got to move on."

"I'm learning the piano," he said. "I'm learning it for you."

The line went dead. He pulled the phone from his ear to stare at the contact photo that popped up for a moment before vanishing. She was smiling, sipping a cocktail at the bar. He hadn't taken it, but rather, she'd sent it to him when they started dating. He threw his phone across the room and onto his bed, where it bounced a few times before getting lost in the sheets.

As much as he felt angry by the rejection, he didn't

feel upset. In fact, his mind instead wandered to Lystra. Though she was a ghost, he felt a stronger connection to her than he had ever felt with Anita. He ran a hand through his hair. What would happen if Lystra decided that he was a lost cause? Would he be able to live with that?

He didn't dream at all that night, and yet somehow, he awoke feeling more tired than before.

FIVE

As the days went by, Colton found himself being drawn more and more toward Lystra, until thoughts of Anita were nearly gone entirely. Every so often, he experienced waves of regret and sadness, but they were becoming less prominent.

"Not like *that*," Lystra said, swatting toward him. "You're making a mockery of my song. Try again."

Colton's eyes were bloodshot, and he yawned. They'd been playing for five hours straight, and all he wanted was sleep. "My hands are cramping up. If you want me to go again, let me take a break."

"You think *I* took breaks while learning?" Lystra's temper was rising. This man was immature. She didn't know how she could have ever expected him to be able to play her song, let alone do it justice. "You think I take breaks *now?*"

"Please? Just five minutes."

"Three." Lystra knew she was being petty, but didn't care. If he wanted her to teach him to play the piano, he would listen to and abide by *her* rules.

Colton rushed to the kitchen and poured his fourth cup of coffee that evening. He sipped it, cupping both his hands around the warm mug, delighting in the way it eased his joints. "I don't know how anyone can play for hours on end without wanting to quit."

"Practice," Lystra said. She thought it was obvious, but added, "it's all practice, in the end. Over time, your hands get used to the way they rest upon the keys. They build up strength and stamina, just like your lungs would if you trained for a marathon."

"It makes sense," he admitted. "But still. You pianists don't get enough credit."

"It's the same with any instrument," she said, running her palms over the wooden lid. She wasn't being humble; she was telling the truth. "Guitarists deal with strings that cut up their fingers, singers have to work around strained vocals, and drummers worry about their hearing. Anything worth doing causes at least some sort of pain."

A question popped into Colton's head, and he said it before he could second guess how it would make her feel. "Can *you* still feel pain?" He didn't like the idea of her being in a state of constant agony.

There was a long, empty silence. "Not in a physical sense. And please, don't pry."

"Okay."

She nodded, and that was that.

Colton sat down the near-empty mug onto the counter and went back over to the piano, sitting down on the stool and cracking his knuckles. "Can you show me one more time?"

She started from the middle. The notes climbed and climbed and climbed, until they came crashing down in a wave of emotion and feeling. It almost sounded like the music was laughing and crying at the same time. And with a flurry of noise, she finished.

"Alright," he said. The first few times she'd played the part for him, he hadn't been able to focus on the notes individually. But now, he *saw* the music instead of just hearing it.

He decided to start from the beginning. It always worked out better that way.

Four notes erupted from his hands, then the next four, and the next. Until both hands were moving on their own accord. He barely thought of what to do before he did it, and simply sat back and watched while his fingers did all the work. He threw his head back and laughed, the sound echoing through the room and sending a smile to Lystra's face.

When the music reached its ascent, she held her breath. Sweat gleamed on his brow, but he didn't hesitate. His hands went faster and faster until they were flesh-toned blurs across the keys.

And then, somehow nearly as perfect as Lystra herself, he let the music drop and fade toward the end.

Lystra's mouth hung open. "You did it," she whispered. Then louder, "Colton, you did it!"

He let out a sound between a laugh and a sob. "I did it."

"Colton, that was it! *You did it!*"

"*We* did it," he corrected. "You're the genius who created this masterpiece. And I—I think I understand the meaning now. It's about love, isn't it?"

"Why do you say that?" He was right, of course, but she was curious to know what his thought process was.

"It starts off very slow, but intense. The two hands

are out of sync, but they work together as two pieces to a puzzle. Then, as the music builds and builds, they become more together. And, at the peak, they're exactly together. Working in tangent. The only thing is, I don't understand the ending. After it all crashes, the two become completely disorganized and play different tunes. What does that represent?"

Never more than at that moment did Lystra wish she was alive so she could throw her arms around his neck and embrace him tightly. She hadn't felt this way in, well, a *very* long time. "I always thought of it as a difficult decision made by one of the lovers. Which relates to how hard it is to get right, I suppose. I personally didn't give much thought to a story beyond its feeling. I like leaving it up to interpretation."

"I think it's beautiful," he said, staring into her eyes and holding the stare.

"Do you want to go through it again?" She couldn't stand looking at his face and not being able to touch him, not being able to feel the warmth of his skin. Another cruelty of being on this Earth but not a part of it. She was just a spectator, allowed to watch but not participate.

"Together?"

"What do you mean?"

He shuffled over on the stool to make room for her.

"I'll play the normal version, and you add some higher notes. What do you think?"

She shrugged, feigning nonchalance. "We could give it a shot." She sat down next to him and rolled her shoulders out of habit. She'd never thought of adding another set of hands before. It was quite brilliant.

He counted them down, and suddenly, the song was filling the air, but this time, with more layers and depth than he could've ever imagined. They worked beautifully together, as if they'd known each other their entire lives.

No further than the first dozen or so notes, and there was a horrible sound from inside the body of the piano. Colton flinched, his hands flying from the keys and behind his back. "What was that?"

If it were possible, Lystra would have gone whiter than she was. She sat there, her wide eyes fixated upon the piano.

Colton said her name, but she didn't hear it. He said it again, and she slowly turned her head to look at him. "What's wrong?"

When she didn't answer, he stood and put his hand atop the lid, bracing himself to push it open.

"Don't!" she screeched. She reached out a hand to grab his arm, but as always, her ghostly figure passed right through him. "Don't look in there?"

"Why?" There was a long pause. "Lystra, talk to me."

"Just, don't."

"Well, I have to fix it if we're going to keep going with our practice. I'm so close to perfection, and you want to stop now?"

She stayed completely still apart from her mouth, which quivered with every word she managed. "You can get another piano."

"Don't be ridiculous," he said with a sigh, and heaved the lid up. He peered inside. "It looks like one of the strings is broken. Do you know how to fix it?" She didn't answer. "Lystra?"

But Lystra was gone. He spun around, looking around the room for any sign of where she could hide. He let out a long breath of air.

"Can you come out? I've never done this before, so some direction would be nice." When still, there was nothing, he dropped the lid and slammed his hand upon the wooden surface in frustration. He didn't understand why she couldn't just tell him what to do.

His phone found its way into his hand, and he looked up the number to a repair company. He surely wasn't about to attempt doing this by himself. Knowing his luck, he'd find a way to break it more.

The phone rang for a while, but then it went to voicemail. He checked the clock on the wall, and mentally slapped himself. It was midnight; of course, they weren't going to answer. Piano repair wasn't exactly a service that needed a night shift.

"Should I take out the string myself?" he asked the piano, hoping Lystra would answer. Even though she didn't say anything, he knew exactly what her answer would be. "You're right. It's probably not a good idea."

And so, he called the number back and left a message explaining what he needed. He was almost tempted to add a joke at the end, but refrained from doing so.

"Not all of us can hide from our problems," he pointed out. "So, if you could come out and face your issues like an adult, that would be great."

But of course, she couldn't be bothered with acting like an adult when she had lived for an eternity.

CHAPTER
SIX

A SINGULAR CANDLE FLICKERED IN THE NIGHT, sitting upon the lid and dripping hot wax onto the tray. Colton sat before it, his hands upon the keys and softly playing her song.

"Lystra, please come out."

There wasn't an answer. There hadn't been one for days.

"I'm starting to believe I imagined you the entire time." This was a lie, of course. His memories felt so real. There was no way his brain could have thought up something like that, or even teach himself a song as complex as hers. "I can't do this without you."

The candle flickered, but he wasn't sure if it was from her or a draft in the room. Both were equally as likely at this point.

Lystra hid, even as Colton kept attempting to coax her out of her piano. She wasn't even sure she could come out if she wanted to; she had buried so deep within herself that she could barely hear his voice. The previous memory of pain had dulled long ago, but now the scab was ripped open to produce a huge, gaping wound. She wasn't sure if this one would ever heal.

Colton hit random notes on the piano and sang out in a terrible voice, *"Lystra, you're my everything."*

It wasn't amusing. In fact, she should have felt insulted by the attempt.

"If you don't show yourself in ten seconds, I will leave."

Good. She wanted him to go, and take his muttering with him

Once the ten seconds passed, he sighed and pushed himself upright. "I'm going upstairs. If you need me, just... play or something."

When he left, she drowned in the silence. Nothing

but the soft hum of air conditioning filled that house. Her fingers itched for the music, but she refrained. Music had killed her, so why did she continue loving it so much?

Perhaps she was foolish to ever hold onto her dream. She wished, then, to simply let go. Forget about the entire thing, and simply vanish to go... wherever her soul would end up. She hadn't exactly gotten far enough to find that out.

It was simply not fair that she died at a young age, unable to experience life or living. She didn't get the luxury of a finish, simply an end that didn't make sense. She never found out what became of her previous lover. While she wished for his happiness, her heart squeezed at the thought of him settling down with a different woman. She couldn't bear the thought of him dying old with a different family surrounding and loving him.

But at least, she had Colton. Or did she? Sure, he was infuriating sometimes, but he had a fire that she'd never seen in anyone else before. Although, he *could* see her, and what did that mean, exactly? Surely, not anything good.

If only Thomas had been able to see her.

Waves of memories washed over Lystra before she could stop them. Memories of them laughing, dancing, singing. He was supposed to be hers forever, and she his. She wasn't supposed to die before the age of thirty, perpetually stuck in time while the world moved on without her.

She wasn't supposed to die.

"I've changed my mind." Colton's voice traveled as he stormed back downstairs. He only stopped when he reached her piano. "You're not going to make me feel insane for talking to a piano. I won't allow that. I got the string fixed; so, what's the issue?"

She didn't — or rather, couldn't — answer. Not yet.

"Is this some sort of ghost thing? Since I added a new part and got rid of the old one, does that mean you're gone now?"

If only it were that easy.

"Because, if you really think about it, if you replace every single part of this piano with pieces of different ones, would it still be the same piano? And thus, would your spirit still attach itself to it? So, by that logic, what's the old-to-new ratio that a ghost needs to exist within its original place? Does time factor in?" He was rambling, but he didn't know what else to do or say.

She didn't know. She didn't care enough to figure it out. There were so many things that still didn't make sense.

"Just give me a sign. One sign that you're still here. That's all I ask — to know you're still here, and I'm not wasting my time trying to talk to you."

She tried, but she simply didn't have the effort to form a body. Maybe she'd try while he slept, send a dream to him through her own. She knew it worked, as she'd tried so many times before to communicate to different people.

"Please, Lystra. Please."

She made the equivalent of an exhale, and snuffed out the wick from the singular candle in the room.

Colton stared at it for a few moments, and then picked it up off the piano. "Thank you."

CHAPTER
SEVEN

Colton went to work the next morning. He still hadn't heard anything from Lystra beyond that candle from the night before. He decided he would give her the space she so clearly wanted. Perhaps, he would spend the night at a hotel and allow her to figure things out for herself. He'd left the television on, as he always had, though he doubted she would deign to watch it.

He stopped himself. He wouldn't allow her to kick him out of his own house. She would have to face him and explain herself.

Colton walked down the familiar sidewalk toward the office building. Since he didn't like to pay for parking, he had about a three blocks' worth of a trek before he reached his work. He didn't mind the walk; it often allowed him to clear his head.

The buildings around were all tall and close together. The streets swarmed with life, as did the sidewalks. He pushed his way through the small crowds, trying to peer over everyone's heads to locate his work building. Although he was running slightly behind, he was sure his boss wouldn't mind. He had been notoriously on time for the past seven years; he was sure that one time wouldn't make a difference.

When he saw it, he almost walked right by. He skidded to a stop, throwing off a young couple behind him, who had to step around quickly to avoid crashing into him. A laminated flier was posted on the window of a convenience store. He walked up the three steps, but didn't have any intention of going inside. He stared at the words and read it over three times in his head.

Think your original song has what it takes? Come to

A&E Recording Studio to try your luck! Top three winners will be featured in our next album...

Colton shook his head. He didn't have a song of his own to showcase. And besides, he wasn't confident yet to perform Lystra's for her.

He continued down the street, quickening his pace to make up for the time lost when he stopped. There was about a minute left until his shift started, and he was still two minutes from the front doors.

As he grew nearer toward the front door, his heart started hammering inside his ears. Anita's voice echoed in his head. *"You're useless. All you do is go to that boring job you have, go home, watch television, and go to bed. I cheated on you because I need something different, Colton."*

Boring. Boring. Boring.

Anita wanted something different. Someone who had a hobby and a great job. She wanted someone to pay attention to her and take her out.

Suddenly, he didn't feel like that was too far out of reach. He had a hobby now, and he could learn to pay more attention. He would work on himself, take her out more, and be a better boyfriend.

He just needed a different job.

Colton paused with his hand upon the front door of the office building. Inside, he saw the reception area, where an older woman named Donna sat, eating pretzels out of a bowl and flipping through her magazine.

He wasn't the kind of man to work an office job. Not anymore.

Before he could decide otherwise, he spun around on his heel and started walking back down the street with a new sense of vigor. He'd show her exactly what kind of man he was willing to be for her.

Lystra, though she was everything to him, was dead. Anita was here; she was his future. He couldn't let her go without a fight.

The flier was in exactly the same place as he'd left it. He noted the details at the bottom, typing the address into the map on his phone. It was only a block over; he didn't even need to drive.

His palms turned sweaty, and he wiped them on his black jeans. He was luckily wearing formal enough office attire that he wouldn't stick out too much. He just hoped that they'd like his music enough to sign him on. If they asked him to create another piece, he could simply take songwriting classes. How hard could it be?

When he rounded the corner, his heart skipped at the long line leading up to A&E Recording Studio. People of all ethnicities and backgrounds were waiting, patiently holding guitars, flutes, and other various instruments. Many people were practicing or tuning, which filled the street with disorganization.

"You in line for the contest?" a young man asked, holding a stack of clipboards in his arm. He was completely casual, with baggy jeans and an oversized plaid shirt.

"Uh... yes," Colton said, pocketing his phone and reaching out for a handshake.

The man grabbed his hand and shook it once, firm. "My name's Steve. Amy and Evelynn own the building, and they'll be interviewing everyone one at a time. Join the queue, and take a clipboard. It's just a questionnaire we ask everyone to get their information. I'll come around in a few minutes if you have any questions."

The man gave Colton a clipboard with a pen attached by a string, and moved onto the woman who had lined up behind him.

He stepped formally into the back of the line, right behind a large, burly man who cradled a small ukulele in his arms. He brought the clipboard up and looked at the sheet. It was fairly standard for a contest form; it asked his name, email, phone number, and various other personal details. At the bottom was a simple waiver, which Colton read thoroughly before signing.

On the back, was a liability form declaring that the song to be showcased must be completely original and composed by the artist performing it. He hesitated, but ultimately put his signature there, too.

Almost as soon as he was done, his pocket started vibrating. He pulled it out, and saw that his boss was trying to contact him. With a deep sigh, he answered.

"Colton! Where are you? You were supposed to be here ten minutes ago." Her sharp voice demanded.

He took a deep breath. This was his moment, and he couldn't back out now. "I quit."

"Are you kidding? You've got to be kidding."

He shuffled back and forth on his feet. "I'm not kidding."

"What is it? Do you want a raise? Or did you get yourself into a jam? You can take vacation days, Colton."

"I quit!" he repeated, his tone growing bolder. "I can't keep working there anymore."

He ended the call and blocked the number before shoving his phone back into his pocket. Somehow, he felt lighter. The world seemed clearer. A giant burden had just been lifted off his shoulders for the first time in seven years.

Had he really hated his job that much?

"I can take that from you," Steve's voice called out, and Colton looked up. He couldn't help but grin, which caused Steve to raise an eyebrow. He took the clipboard and looked over all the answers. "Alright,

Colton. We've already started the first set of people, but your wait is looking at about forty minutes, give or take."

Colton nodded; he didn't mind waiting. In fact, it would give him time to ease his nerves before he went inside. "Do you guys have a piano I can use? It'd be a bit hard to bring my own."

"Oh, absolutely," Steve said. "We have almost every type of instrument there is, but many people choose to bring their own if they can."

When Colton assured the man that he had no more questions, Steve left to chat with the woman in line behind him.

"You like the piano? How long have you been playing?" The burly man in front of him asked.

"Oh, not very long, I guess," Colton said. He didn't want to tell the man that it had only been a couple weeks. He felt like it would discredit his newfound talent. "How about you?"

"Since I was young," he said, flipping his ukulele over in his hands. "My whole family has musical talent, so they had me start early."

Colton became overwhelmed after that statement. He knew he was good. Lystra had told him so, but how many of the people in this line had been playing their whole life? What if he had quit his job, lost all security, for nothing?

His attention was snagged by two women speaking behind him.

"—heard they're *really* tough," the one said, her voice high and lilting. "My coworker tried once, and said they were so brutal she cried afterwards."

The other girl responded, "it can't be *that* bad. Remember they hired Willow Phillips that one time? Can't get much lower than that."

He hoped the second girl was right. He *needed* this. Not just for his sake, but for Anita's, too. So, she could finally see him like she was always supposed to.

"You play the flute, right? What about you?"

"I was thinking piano at first, but they hear a *lot* of pianists come through all the time, and I don't want mine to get all mixed up with theirs. So, I'm just singing."

"Good plan."

None of this was easing Colton's nerves at all, so he tried his best to tune them out and pulled out his phone. He scrolled through until he found one of the games he'd downloaded a long time ago to play during his breaks. It was boring and uninteresting. Perfect.

The forty minutes somehow passed too quickly but not fast enough.

Colton stepped up to the front doors, where Steve waved him forward. The record studio looked small on the outside, but the moment Colton stepped over the threshold, he marveled at how well the entire thing was laid out. Couches lined the walls, with low coffee tables available for social gatherings. It was incredibly cozy, something his previous job had never been.

"Right back here," Steve said, and Colton stepped through a door labeled, "Quiet Room."

He went inside, and Steve closed the door behind him. He looked around, and despite four enclosed walls and a large glass window, it looked like a stage. Different instruments lined the walls, including a drum set and a keyboard. Microphone stands littered the area, only about half holding actual microphones.

"Colton, right?" a woman's voice called over a speaker in the room. He looked through the glass to see the owner of the voice and one other sitting on large, green couches.

"Yes," he said, sitting down on the stool before the keyboard.

A stout, blonde-haired woman wrote something onto what Colton recognized to be his clipboard. "I'm Evelynn, and that's Amy. We'll be in charge of judging you today. What's your song called?"

He froze. He had never heard Lystra refer to it as anything other than her song. "I haven't created a name for it yet."

The brunette, tall and skinny despite sitting down, asked, "and what's the genre?"

"Instrumental?" He cleared his throat. "Classical instrumental."

Amy flicked a switch, and everything on the other side of the glass became muted.

Calming his breathing the best he could, Colton walked over to the keyboard and sat down. He was used to the older, wooden piano at his house, but this one would do. He just had to remember those first four notes.

His hands froze inches above the keys. What *were* the first four notes? His heart hammered in his chest. He couldn't remember, couldn't think of how the song could fathomably start.

"Anytime now." Amy's voice chuckled slightly.

Colton took a deep breath and cleared his mind. His fingers would know what to do, if only he could remember those first four notes.

He played the first note, then the second, and the third. But when his finger went to press the fourth note, his sweaty hand slipped and hit the completely wrong note.

"I—I'm sorry," Colton stuttered out. "Can I try again?"

"Go ahead," Amy said. "It's not easy to play in front of an audience."

Colton stared at the keyboard for another few

moments. But then — he could almost see it there, in his mind, Lystra's fingers atop his own.

"*Like this,*" she would have said if she were here. "*You can do it. You're just freezing up.*"

His fingers launched into the song. As soon as those first four notes went by, he remembered exactly what to do. A shudder went down his spine, but he kept going. He reached the crescendo, bringing the notes higher and higher, faster and faster. He could almost feel Lystra's presence, laughing while he played.

And then the music, as it always did, came crashing down and slid to a halt.

Colton looked up and out the window toward the two women. Amy's eyes were wide, her mouth gaping open. Evelynn's brows were drawn together. She flipped a switch, and the audio played over the speaker.

Evelynn asked, "how long have you been writing music?"

Colton shrugged. "This song has been in the works for a long time. It just recently got perfected enough to play in front of someone."

"That's incredible," Amy said. "Truly. I've never really been a fan of classical music, but this has exceeded all expectations."

"Really?" Colton asked, beaming. "Do you think I've made the top three?"

"Top *three*?" Evelynn said. "To hell with the top three. I'm pretty sure you've just made the top, period."

Colton let out a shaky breath. Tears brimmed in his eyes. "Thank you! I... this just means a lot. Thank you."

"Steve will take you into the waiting area. We still have to get through all the other contestants, but as far as we're concerned, the deal is yours."

Colton couldn't believe his ears. Sure, he knew Lystra's song had been good, but he didn't realize it was *this* good. And he had played it well.

Steve came in and led him out into the couched waiting area. He sat down on the red leather sofa, one leg crossed over the other. He could certainly get used to being a musician. He took his phone from his pocket and dialed a number. Surprisingly, the person hadn't blocked him yet.

"Hey, Anita. No, don't hang up. You'll never guess what just happened."

CHAPTER
EIGHT

When Colton walked in through his front door, Lystra was there. She greeted him with a smile, gesturing for him to follow her toward the living room.

"Lystra—"

"Come, come! While you were gone at work, I thought about your idea. The one about playing it together. I think it could work, but I need to hear you play it so I can form my half of the melody."

"You were gone," he snapped. "You left for days. What happened?"

She flinched at the words. "I'm sorry. When the string snapped, it brought back horrible, terrible memories that I've fought for a long, long time to be rid of."

"That doesn't excuse anything." Colton walked past her, brushing aside her pleas of protest.

"I said I'm sorry! Does that mean anything to you?"

He stopped in the middle of the room and clutched his hair between his fingers. He just needed time to think, to figure this whole thing out.

"Is this about practice time being lost? It's only a few days; it doesn't matter that much. We can make it up this weekend."

"I don't need your instruction anymore," Colton snapped, heading over toward the piano in the corner of the room. "In fact, I don't even think we need this anymore."

Lystra was taken aback. "Don't *need* it? Colton, you know that I'm tied to this piano. Wherever it goes, I go."

He didn't say anything. Sizing up the wooden piece of furniture as if it were nothing but an old cabinet he never liked, Colton placed his hands on his hips. He wasn't sure how, but he was going to get it out of his house.

"I thought you were doing well, and now all of a sudden, you don't want to play anymore?" It didn't make sense, and she was trying to get it all to make sense.

Colton shook his head, laughing to himself. "You don't get it."

"Talk to me!" Lystra screamed, floating in front of him and baring her teeth.

The way he stared at her with complete distaste unnerved her. It was like he didn't see *her*, but rather, some mildly interesting creature. She couldn't stand it.

"I'm not afraid of you," Colton said, his voice almost completely nonchalant.

Her face fell. "You... I wasn't trying to scare you."

He let out a singular, dry chuckle. "You're a ghost. It's what ghosts do. I just... I need you to go, Lystra."

The words stung as if he'd slapped her. "What about our deal?" She was pleading at this point. For the first time in her life, she was pleading with a man. Then, she added in a whisper, "what about us?"

"What about it?" He finally looked at her, but there was nothing of the man she had grown to love. "There was never anything between us. Maybe friendship, but nothing else."

She was shattered. Everything she had built and

worked hard to maintain for so long was being torn down by a few sentences from this man.

"Look, Anita is coming over soon, and I want you gone before then. I've ordered a new piano, so don't worry about me falling behind on my lessons."

"What did I do?" She was almost yelling at this point. She had finally, *finally*, met someone who could see her, who wasn't afraid. She thought he had understood her, related to her. She thought they were friends, at the very least.

"—NEW SONG BY COLTON BRODIE HAS CAPTURED the world's hearts. Despite only having been out for a few hours, A&E Recording Studio has sold out." A reporter's voice came from the television, the same one Colton had left on before he left that morning. "In case you haven't heard it, we'll play it for you now."

And then it started. Lystra's song began playing over the television speakers.

She turned around slowly to face the screen. She couldn't believe it. Her song was playing. The melody was being heard by people across the world.

So, why was she still here?

"And there you go! Colton's song, currently titled, *Love, Anita...*"

"Now, don't get mad," Colton said, raising his palms toward the ghost woman before him. "I get that we had a deal, but really, I did what you said. I put your song out into the world. It's not my fault that they think I wrote it."

She was beyond angry. Something between wrath and fury consumed every thought, and all she saw was red. He was supposed to tell the world that *she* wrote it. It was *her* song, not his.

"For what it's worth, I'm sorry," he said, watching as she settled into a deadly calm. "But you have to go now. I'm sure someone very nice will come pick you up. Maybe they'll be able to see you, too."

She screamed. The sound was completely paranormal, and Colton threw his hands over his ears to block out the sound. "How could you do this to me?" she shouted, rushing toward him and through his body. He fell over, the cold, numb feeling spreading from his chest to the rest of his body.

He choked and coughed, sputtering as he rolled over and pushed himself upright. "Don't start this, Lystra."

"*You* started this." Her voice echoed all around him without a body. "You took the one thing I still had away from me. I trusted you, and you betrayed me!"

He rushed toward the hall closet, where he pulled out his mop. "I said I was sorry!"

"Sorry doesn't bring back my song, does it?!" She appeared in front of him, and he swung at her with the mop. She evaded his swing and flew to his side, where she thrust a hand inside his head and left it there.

Colton cried out in pain, falling to his knees. It initially felt like brain-freeze, but then started to burn. When she pulled her hand away, his head throbbed and his mind spun.

"You don't touch my piano. Go and fix what you've done. Tell the world that it's my song, and then we'll talk."

Colton's hand gripped the mop handle harder, and he shook his head. "That can't happen."

She rushed for him again, but this time, he was expecting it. He stepped out of the way and ran over to the piano. He brought the mop handle down on it once, twice, three times.

"Stop!" Lystra yelled, putting herself between Colton and her beloved instrument. He kept hitting the piano over and over again until the wood began to splinter off, spraying shards in every direction. He ignored her when she grabbed at his hand, trying to get him to drop the mop. She kicked through his torso, but he gritted his teeth through the cold, searing pain.

Abandoning the mop, he grabbed the piano and started hauling it across the floor. Lystra screamed profanities and threats toward him, but he didn't let it faze him. He reminded himself that she was just a ghost, and couldn't actually touch him.

He threw the piano out the door, and it slid down the steps. One of the legs snapped off when it landed on the concrete in a heap. Now on its side, Colton hauled it to the end of the driveway. When he was finished, he dusted off his hands and glared at Lystra one last time before heading inside.

When Colton left, her anger turned to grief. She sobbed uncontrollably, sitting atop her battered piano that was tipped on its side. Not only was the last thing she cared about ripped from her, now her home was shattered, too. Nobody would want a broken piano, and so she'd inevitably end up in some sort of dumpster. Maybe she'd be incinerated, and everything would have been for nothing.

At least then, she'd be free of all this nonsense.

CHAPTER
NINE

Lystra sat there for an insurmountable amount of time. It had started to rain, first in tiny droplets that thudded against the wood in rapid, trepidatious intervals. But as the hour went on, they started falling faster, harder. Until the entire piano was soaked, and the ground flooded in wide, sloshing puddles.

And though Lystra could not feel, she could have sworn a chill went down her spine. She could almost experience the looming cold as if she were back alive with a physical form.

At some point, a young woman arrived in a flashy silver car. She pulled into the driveway and stepped out into the rain, opening up an umbrella to protect her soft curls from the water. Her heels clicked against the driveway as she bolted up toward the front door.

She knocked twice before Colton appeared, smiling broadly as he embraced the woman. Lystra felt a pang of jealousy shoot through her, and she glared with her ghostly form.

"What's with the piano at the end of the driveway?" She heard the woman ask.

Colton waved it off. "Broken. I bought a keyboard instead."

They went inside, but not before Colton shot Lystra a cold look over the woman's shoulder.

She could only watch through the window in reluctant longing as the man she had previously thought would solve everything sat down at his new keyboard and played. He played for the young woman whose name Lystra didn't care to remember. She didn't *want* to remember.

She knew what was keeping her from finally moving on to the life after this. If there was such a thing. She knew, but was powerless to sever the angry ties that kept her rooted on this Earth with no body, no physical essence. Just a thinking, pitiful soul that just wanted to be loved.

She *had* been loved, once. By a man whom she loved back dearly. They were supposed to have a life, they were supposed to grow old together, and one day tell their grandkids about the song they wrote together. Thomas had plans to propose to her, she'd found out much later. But she never got to see the recipient of his grandmother's heirloom. She hoped he had found that love again, even if it squeezed her heart to think about it.

But instead, she was killed, and ended up eternally trapped within the thing that ended her life.

At some point, she wasn't sure when, she took to screaming at the passing vehicles. None saw her, of course, but it got out the anger and frustration she felt.

As cars of all types and sizes soared past in the rain, spraying waves of water onto her piano, Lystra couldn't help but expel every bit of anger she felt onto the living. It was her fault for trusting someone, but it was greed and betrayal that had caused her to feel this way. She didn't understand these incredibly mortal emotions.

But then, there was a man. And Lystra thought he looked incredibly familiar as he drove past, stopped, and reversed in front of the driveway. He hopped out of the truck and, not seeing Lystra, placed a hand atop the piano.

He was handsome, with shaggy brown hair and a well-built figure. Her eyes snagged on his hands, which were long and slender, yet calloused and scarred from years of use.

"Who would treat a beautiful antique like this?" he whispered to himself, his fingers lightly brushing against the wood. His voice was as beautiful as he was. "You don't deserve this."

She wanted to shout at him, tell him that she doesn't know either, but she couldn't. She didn't say a word, holding her breath at the familiarity of this man. Where had she seen him before?

The man's perfect green eyes shot straight through Lystra and to Colton's house. He thought for a few minutes before rushing back to his truck and grabbing some ratchet straps. He couldn't, in good conscience, leave the piano behind for the dump to collect and smash it into smithereens. It simply wouldn't sit well with him.

It didn't take long for him to maneuver the piano onto the back of the truck. Using the straps for leverage and his own sheer muscle, it only took him a couple tries to push it onto the bed. The entire time, he was incredibly gentle. Not one extra scratch marred the wood when he was finished.

He secured a navy-blue tarp on top of the piano, then fastened it down with the straps. He gave it a test pull and, satisfied, climbed into the front of the truck. Lystra thought that the tarp was unnecessary, seeing how it was completely soaked already. She appreciated the care, however, and flew into the back to sit atop her covered piano.

Things didn't seem quite so cold anymore.

Lystra watched as Colton's house got smaller and smaller in the distance, and when they rounded a corner, broke down into tears.

CHAPTER
TEN

The man talked to himself a lot. Lystra didn't mind, as she could pretend at times that he was speaking to her, and she would answer back with her own responses. It was a great comfort to her as he started working on fixing the piano.

"I'm not sure I want to know what happened," he said for the umpteenth time that afternoon. "I mean, throwing out a beautiful piece like this onto the street? Absurd!" He wasn't sure why the piano had been tossed in the first place. Apart from the water damage and broken pieces of wood that surely came after it had been dumped, it was in perfect condition. He knew quite a bit about pianos from his grandfather, who religiously cleaned and cared for the instruments he owned.

"Respect your equipment, and it'll pay with good music," he always told him.

"I agree," Lystra said, lounging atop the off-balance piano and twirling her finger as if stirring a martini. One of the legs had snapped, and he was trying to properly balance and fix that before starting on the rest of the body. As his hands worked, he kept the sound of the radio in the background for some noise.

"You know... I got a piano for my grandfather. He used to play, though I don't remember him very well. He used to tell me stories about his own father, who pushed him into lessons very young."

This was the longest phrase he'd ever said, and Lystra said nothing. She didn't want to ruin anything. She shifted in her position as he lifted the piano higher to put the foot back on.

"But he passed away last month. I got the house, and my sister got anything valuable within. She sold most of it, including his gorgeous antique grand piano.

I planned on buying a new one sometime this week, but you found me first. You feel like you match this house, you know?"

That was quite possibly the best compliment she had ever received.

"There, that should do it." He stood up and placed the level atop different surfaces. Wherever he placed it, the bubble remained solely in the middle. Lystra cheered along with him. "I just have to recheck the strings..."

She held her nonexistent breath as he opened the lid and reached inside, testing the strings for weaknesses. She couldn't bear to watch, but she couldn't look away. He checked the tune and integrity of each, making sure none required cleaning or replacing.

Thankfully, nothing terribly devastating happened to him, and he stepped back. He closed the lid, then dusted off his hands. "Remarkably in alright condition. I think after a fresh coat of sealant, you'll be good as new."

Something close to happiness swelled in her chest. The man left sometime after, presumably to get the "sealant" that he had mentioned.

During this time, she roamed around the house. It was beautiful, though empty. The man's sister must have found a lot she deemed valuable. She had left family photos, however, which were propped up in random spots all over the house and lined the main hallway.

Kids, grandkids, and families. She learned that the man's name was Oliver, but what snagged her attention was the surname written on the bottom of some photos along with the dates: Bennett.

She'd never forget that last name, because it was supposed to be hers.

Thomas Bennett had been her lover, her everything. And now, here was his great-grandson, by complete chance.

She fell to her knees when she saw his face.

Thomas. It was him, only much, much older. She had spent long hours throughout her life imagining what he'd look like older. He had a pretty girl by his side, and a couple grandkids. The one son was undoubtedly Oliver's grandfather, as it was clearly his house.

Her Thomas' kids had lived here. That meant that, at some point, Thomas himself had likely walked these halls. Had he thought of her at all into his elder years? Had he forgotten her completely?

Her fingers caressed the frame, and she longed to go back to the days when she could feel something, anything at all.

When Oliver came home, she tried desperately to get his attention. She tried shouting, waving her arms, grabbing onto him, anything that would usually get people to realize she was there. But perhaps, Oliver was more mentally sound than the others she had been around, or he genuinely did not see her there.

When the piano was finished, her mouth dropped open. It hadn't looked this good since she first got it so many years ago. A gift from her parents when she decided that music was to be her passion, her life's work. It hadn't been expensive, by any means, but it was hers. And now, it was new.

Oliver went off to bed, and Lystra was antsy. She couldn't let this be the end; she had to communicate with him. Tell him that she was here, who she was. She couldn't explain why, but it was incredibly important to her that he knew. That he recognized her for what she was and...

She didn't know what she would do after. After Oliver knew that there was a ghost woman living in his piano who also used to be with his great-grandfather — then what? Talk about it?

Still, it was worth a shot.

Using the ability she had discovered long ago, she slipped into his dream. She felt bad for doing it, as nightmares were always terrible windows into her pain and suffering, but she couldn't figure out another way to communicate.

IT ALL STARTED AND ENDED WITH LONELINESS.

A young girl stood there, amongst her elderly mother and father. They looked as if they could be her grandparents, and smiled wide at their perfect little miracle.

But the girl aged into a beautiful young woman, whose face turned yellow and sickly. She looked wrong; she looked—

The dream shifted, and she was standing, her face twisted in a horrible scream. Oliver was powerless to watch in his body-that-wasn't-a-body as she collapsed to the ground, convulsing before she died.

His grandfather was there — no, this man was much too tall to be his grandfather. His great-grandfather then. He stared down at this woman in horrible pain with tears in his eyes. Oliver felt his pain, and wanted to comfort his relative. But he had no body, and he could not speak.

The voices were muffled, but he could make out words such as "love" and "remember." His great-grandfather kissed the woman on the forehead, and both of them disappeared.

His entity floated into an abyss of nothingness. Blinding-white nothingness that put him on edge. Where was he supposed to go? What was he supposed to *do? Why did he have no body, no essence, no physical form to move?*

Oliver began to panic. He cried out for help, but there were no ears for his words to reach.

What to do, what to do, what to do—

OLIVER WOKE UP IN A COLD SWEAT AND BOLTED upright in his bed. The sheets were all twisted around his limbs, and he ran his hands over his face. He couldn't comprehend the dream he just had. If he took that to a dream psychologist, what would they have to say about it? What did it *mean*?

It was midnight, as evident by the alarm clock beside his bed. He got up and slipped some pants on, omitting a shirt. He walked into his adjoining bathroom and ran the faucet, throwing water over his face. Oliver stared at himself in the mirror for a few moments before patting his face dry. He didn't often have nightmares, but this somehow felt... real.

He climbed back into bed, and Lystra didn't have the heart to send more nightmares his way.

She had spent her entire existence as a ghost trying desperately *not* to be seen, and now here she was, doing everything in her power to be seen. Perhaps Colton had ruined it for her, but she had enjoyed the human contact for a while. Now, she craved for someone to understand.

Lystra sat down at the piano and watched the man round the corner and go back to sleep. She made the motion of cracking her knuckles, though it wasn't necessary.

Her hands flew over the keys, tentatively hitting the first few notes. Then the next.

Oliver paused. He knew that song, but not because it had been playing on the radio the past couple days. No, he *knew* the song from the deepest dregs of his memory.

He walked over to the piano, not a hint of panic or fright. As if a piano playing itself was the most normal thing in the world. He opened his mouth and sang.

"Oh, love. There you are.

Daisy. Rose. You don't compare.

Oh, love. Please don't leave.

I must stop and stare."

Tears fell freely from her eyes. She'd never been the singing type, and as such had never truly remembered the lyrics. But she knew these were right; she knew that these were the same words sung in the same voice as Thomas.

More verses, just like that one. Then, as the piano's voice began to rise, so did Oliver's. It was almost as if they had been playing together for years, practicing for decades.

"Don't forget.
Save our love.
Never surrender.
You're my safety.
Nobody compares.
I won't forget.
I will love.
I'll never surrender.
I know safety.
I can't compare."

His voice was lovely; she couldn't deny it. He paused as the music came crashing down, and a singular tear slipped down his face, though he was smiling.

"Oh, love. When will you come?
For what it's worth, I loved you, too.
Oh, love. Please don't leave.
For days — we have few."

The tale was never supposed to be happy; it was never supposed to have a pleasant ending. As was her own life, she understood. She never had something end well for her. Perhaps, even before they created the song together, Thomas understood that. He'd understood her.

"I wonder how that man got his hands on my family song." Oliver breathed after a while. Though he couldn't see her, and she couldn't feel him, they shared that moment in intimate harmony.

"OKAY," OLIVER SAID, HOLDING A HUGE cardboard box filled with his grandfather's things. He was sure they belonged to *his* father, as they were dated sometime around the time he knew his great-grandfather had passed away. "I want you to press a high note for yes and a low note for no. Can you do that?"

Lystra laughed to herself, but pressed the high

note. Only minutes after they had finished their song, he'd rushed off to the attic to collect anything and everything he could on the family song that had been passed down through generations.

He sat down on the floor, taking the lid off the box and peering in. "First, are you a ghost?"

She rolled her eyes. Her finger hit the high note, and held it a little bit longer than necessary.

Oliver laughed. "Okay, okay, no need to be sarcastic about it. Just had to ask."

He pulled out a photograph. It was of Thomas as a younger man. Memories flooded her mind, but she shook them away. Thomas was gone, but here was Oliver, and he was trying to help.

"This is my great-grandfather. Did you know him?"

High note.

"Did he write the song you played last night?"

She hesitated. She went to hit the low note, but hesitated. It might send the wrong message. She opted for hitting them alternatingly.

He seemed to understand. "Did you?"

High note.

"Well, it's very well done," he told her. "He died long before I was born, but his son, my grandfather, loved to play."

She didn't do anything because he hadn't asked a

question. She could hardly sit still. It was exciting, communicating with someone this way.

"Are you related to me in any way?"

Low note. She wasn't his great-grandmother, just simply the woman his ancestor had courted a long time ago.

He started rummaging through the box of things, asking various questions to narrow down who she was. Eventually, he got a brilliant idea.

"Do you know Morse code?" he asked, jumping to his feet.

What was that? She hit the low note.

Oliver, just as excited as she was, rushed over to his laptop and pulled it open. After some clicks and typing, there was a whirr on the other side of the room. A sheet of paper slid from the printer, ink blots on it. He grabbed it and propped it up on the ledge where sheet music would go. She saw that each letter corresponded to a dash or a line.

"Dash is a long note; dot is a short one. I did some pilot's training and am fairly fluent. Go on, give it a try. What's your name?"

It took a while for her to get used to whatever this was. She hit the notes for L, then Y, and the rest of her name followed.

"Lisstra," he tried, but butchered at the pronunciation. She hit the low note, and he tried again. "Liestra," he enunciated. She hit the high note, and he smiled. Dimples appeared in the corners of his mouth. "Lystra."

He sorted through the box until he finally came to a newspaper article. She read the title, and furiously hammered at the high note. He hadn't asked a question, but understood what she was trying to say.

"Budding musician, Lystra Flowers, killed in tragic piano accident," he read out. "You were twenty-seven when you passed?"

Sad high note. She loved the minor keys for this reason.

She glanced back at the Morse code sheet. It took a while, but she managed to get out, *"Colton stole song."*

He nodded. "My family thought so, too. But since we weren't sure exactly where the song came from, we didn't know if perhaps we were distant relatives. You're sure he took this song without your permission?"

Yes, she was absolutely certain. The deal had been that he share the song in *her* name.

Besides, he wasn't even ready yet. His fingers were still clunky and hesitating. He hit each note as if he meant it, and not with the softness it deserved.

After a long moment of silence, Oliver asked her, "do you want to do something about it?"

She thought for a moment. She'd been so

consumed by rage and pain that she hadn't thought about that. What could they even do about it? Tell everyone that Colton Brodie stole the song from a ghost, and that the true writer was a ghost that'd been trapped inside a piano for nearly a century? Likely not.

Her finger hit the high note, letting it ring out into the room with a sense of finality. Oliver smiled, showing his top row of perfect white teeth. He grabbed the newspaper from the box, and tore Lystra's picture from the article. He propped it up next to the Morse code sheet.

"So, I feel like I'm not going crazy talking to myself," he told her. "I want to know more about you, about your life."

She explained it as best as she could. The Morse code was clunky at best, and she occasionally got the notes wrong and had to restart. She did love hearing him speak, though. He had a wonderful voice that reminded her so much of Thomas, and it made her chest ache.

"What's family like?" she asked him through the keys. She wanted to know, not only what the Bennett family was like, but also what it meant to have a family at all. She knew her parents would be dead by now, and she didn't have any siblings or children of her own.

"Well, my grandfather was a funny man. He loved the piano and anything comedy. Him and I were really close while I was growing up, even though my grand-mother passed away when I was young. It was just him and I while my father put himself through school and became a lawyer. He told many stories about his own father. Useless around any instrument and — well, you probably know all about Thomas."

A sad high note, followed by a low one. She knew him, and yet she didn't. He was as much a stranger now as anyone could be.

"I'm sorry," Oliver said softly. "My sister has three kids, though. Cute as can be, and little rascals to boot. We all get together for dinner every month or so, and switch up who hosts. And that's about it, really."

As the night went on, she spoke to Oliver through the piano. In just a few short hours, and with much more of a communication barrier, she got to know this wonderful, kind man more intimately than she'd known anyone else in her entire life.

CHAPTER
TWELVE

"You can do this, I promise."

Oliver's encouraging words did nothing to calm Lystra's nerves. She barely refused to come out of the piano, preferring instead to hide within. She wasn't mortal; she shouldn't be nervous.

And yet, she was. She was terrified at the idea of

everything going horribly, terribly wrong. Even though she and Oliver had practiced for hours on end, making his hand movements believable enough to go along with her own playing, she still refused to believe that it could go as planned.

"You're Oliver Bennett, yes?" An official-looking man with a clipboard asked, walking over to him and his piano backstage. "You've... brought your own instrument. We said we'd provide our own."

Oliver didn't miss a beat. "I have a special connection with this piano. I can't play without her."

"Do you mind if we check for any tampering or sound devices?" When Oliver shook his head, the suited man gestured to his men to come forward and look it over.

Lystra refrained from chuckling, and based on Oliver's face, he was, too. Of course, technically, Oliver *was* cheating through her. But they didn't know any of that.

When they were done looking it over, the man straightened and wrote something down on his clipboard. "You're four acts away; make sure you're ready." He glanced up and down at Oliver's rather plain appearance, but didn't say anything before walking away.

"Are you scared?" Oliver asked once they were out of earshot, and sat down at the piano. She hit the high note softly, and he sighed. "Me, too. I've never actually performed in front of an audience before. But we're in this together, right?"

Another high note rang out.

"I'm sorry, but did you just talk to that piano?" a masculine voice asked that was distinctly *not* Oliver's. She bristled, even though she knew he couldn't see her right now.

"Colton Brodie, what a pleasure," Oliver's voice said dryly.

"Just 'Colton' will do." God, how had she ever liked this man? Even his voice was pretentious. The only thing stopping her from rushing out and trying to hurt him again was the fact that they were about to enact revenge upon him. "I've never seen you around before. Are you new?"

"You only started your music career a week ago, and you're saying things like that?" Oliver chuckled. Calm, cool, and collected, nothing would shake him. "Stop trying to fish for points where there aren't any and get lost, kid."

"I'm afraid I can't do that," Colton told him. "See, I'm part of the crew, and I was told to get a set list from everyone."

She wished she could jump out and see Colton's reaction, but she refrained.

"I'm afraid I'm just doing the one song," Oliver

said. "And it's a family song; we never named it officially."

Colton hummed to himself, typing down something into his tablet. "Then give me a work-in-progress title. Oftentimes, labels will change the names of songs anyway, unless you get it really good on the first try. But — I'm sure you know all about that."

He was leaning into Oliver, but Oliver wouldn't budge. He crossed one of his legs over the other. "Actually, I wouldn't. I'm not doing this for fame; I just love my music."

Colton recoiled slightly, and Oliver smiled at him. But not the wide, dimple-grin that he wore around Lystra; no, this was twisted and dared Colton to say something else.

"I'm afraid I'm going to need some sort of title," Colton said, and Lystra had enough.

"Anything's better than *Love, Anita*," Lystra said, appearing next to Oliver.

Colton flinched, staring wide-eyed at the ghostly form next to Oliver, who couldn't see anything.

"Lystra? What the hell are you doing? I—I didn't recognize your piano."

Oliver quirked up an eyebrow, the first sense of surprise he'd shown. "You can see her?"

"Of *course*, I can see her. She's sitting right there!" He splayed out his fingers toward Lystra's form.

Oliver turned and looked, but he couldn't see a thing. "I don't know what you're talking about." He was slightly jealous that this man could see her, and he couldn't, but he reminded himself that Colton wasn't exactly... stable.

"Oh, forget about it. Lys—are you planning on playing *the* song?"

"You mean *my* song?" she asked, baring her teeth. "The song that you *stole*? I don't know. Am I?"

Oliver, having not heard anything on Lystra's side, stared expectantly at Colton, who said, "well, I hope you know I've put a copyright on it already. You can't do anything."

"Copyrights *can* be broken," Oliver answered for her. "And luckily for us, my mother's a lawyer. She's getting ready to sue you as we speak, so I hope you're not attached to all your pretty money." He said all this so casually that it took Colton a few moments for the news to sink in. His face went white.

"You wouldn't." He looked to Lystra, who shrugged. "No... you can't!"

"It's what you get for being an asshole, Colton," Lystra said at the same time Oliver retorted, "We can, and we will."

"Please don't. You're dead! You don't have any need for money or fame or wealth. I'm still living; shouldn't you want my life to be good?"

She shook her head. "I don't care about you anymore. Not since you stole everything I've ever loved."

"Anita will leave me," he muttered softly. "She'll leave me, and I'll be left with nothing"

"If she truly loved you," Oliver said, standing now. "You wouldn't be worried about that."

Colton fell to his knees, chest heaving. Lystra felt a few shreds of pity for him, but not enough to do anything. "Please! It's all I have!"

"It's not even yours," Oliver spared a glance back at Lystra's piano, "so get over yourself. If you want to have a career as a musician, write your own songs."

"I'll be ruined," he sobbed out. "Nobody will take me seriously after this. And — *oh my god*, I quit my job for this!"

"Not my problem. Next time, keep your hands off someone else's work."

"Hey, Bennett?" It was the same guy in a suit as before. "You're up. My guys will take the piano out for you. What are you doing on the floor, Brodie?"

Colton scrambled to his feet and sent Lystra one last pleading look before disappearing through one of the various doors. She didn't have time to say anything to either of them before her and her piano were pulled past the long, black curtains and out onto the stage.

Luckily, the red curtains were still drawn, and she had a few moments to calm her breath.

But Oliver didn't sit down right away. He stood toward the audience when the curtains raised. He splayed out his arms, and she noticed that he was wearing a headset microphone.

"You don't know me. My name is Oliver Bennett, and I've had the pleasure of knowing a very talented young woman. Unfortunately, she passed away, and so I am here to speak on her behalf. Her song, her *stolen* song, has been claimed by someone who doesn't have the right to play it. I'm here to set things right."

She wanted desperately to thank him, to wrap her arms around him and thank him for those kind words. But now was not the time for that, so she settled for the soft brushing of a high note.

"You'll do great," he said and sat down on the stool. It was odd, sharing a space with him, but if he felt the cold, he didn't show it.

Side-profile to the audience, Lystra watched as people whispered amongst each other, trying to figure out what was going on. *People* were in the audience. Actual *people* were here to listen to her play.

Oliver muttered, "one, two, three," and suddenly, Lystra's fingers found the keys, and she was playing. As she went through the first verse on her own, people in the stands continued their muttering. This was the same song that had been going viral this past week, and now, some other man was playing it, claiming it to have been... stolen?

Oliver's hands flew along hers with such precision that she was almost sure he could play it on his own.

And then he started singing. The lyrics melted off his tongue and into the air, completing what was missing from the piece. Verse upon verse of the sweet, sad song.

Then her favorite part came. The ascending melody made her feel as if she had never died at all. As if she were still a young, mortal girl who was experiencing love's painful sting for the first time in her life.

At the peak of the crescendo, Oliver sang out, "*I can't compare.*"

And it all came crashing down.

She might have been crying, she might have been shaking, but her hands didn't once falter on the keys. They knew the song better than she did, and they weren't about to mess it up.

Then, when the song faded off into the air, it was done. It was over. Silence filled the theater.

Applause broke out almost all at once. It was an overwhelming amount of noise and appreciation.

Lystra's heart soared. She'd never felt lighter in all

her life, and she realized that she was floating. Though she yearned to tell Oliver how she truly felt, and desperately wanted to wait and watch how the events of the trial played out, she knew it was time.

And she was free.

EPILOGUE

Oliver sat on the couch, his two little toddlers running around him. His girl always chased the boy, as she was older and hated the way her brother would take her toys. They were perfect little embodiments of love and joy.

Until they inevitably weren't.

"Kids!" he shouted. "Please don't fight each other at seven in the morning. Your mother's still sleeping."

The oldest one cringed. "Sorry, Daddy."

The younger child, only knowing to copy his sister, apologized, too.

"It's not me you have to worry about if you wake your mom. You know she likes her beauty rest."

He watched his kids for a few more minutes before leaning back and flicking on the radio, making sure to turn the dial nearly all the way down. A familiar song filled the air, and he smiled. He always thought of Lystra when her song played. He made a note to always stop whatever he was doing and think about her. Even though he'd only ever met her through a piano, he'd felt closest to her than anyone else in his life.

Until he met his children. His eldest daughter was named Lystra, though they called her Lys most of the time. His wife hadn't known the significance of the name when they chose it, but she had agreed.

"*Oh, love. Please don't leave,*" he muttered, barely singing. But Lys stopped, looking at him with her head tilted to the side.

"What's that, Daddy?"

"*I must stop and stare.*" He smiled at their confused faces. He sat up, rested his arms on his knees, and began to sing softly, in barely a whisper.

It had been so long since he'd sung that song, but the lyrics flowed as if it had been no time at all. It represented so much in his life, and brought back so many memories.

He still remembered the moment he'd realized that she was gone for good. The stage hands had helped carry the piano offstage, and once they were gone, he'd asked Lystra what she thought. But silence followed.

Still, he couldn't bring himself to get rid of the piano. So, it sat in his living room. He planned on putting his children into lessons at some point, the moment they expressed interest in it. He was sure Lystra would have appreciated it.

"What was that song?" Lys asked, her brother obliviously enjoying time without his sister pestering him.

"Have I never told you about where your name comes from?" he asked, and the small child shook her head. "I think you must have been too young."

He took a deep breath.

"You see, a long time ago, there was this beautiful woman named Lystra with an unparalleled talent for music..."

"Telling stories again?" a female voice asked from behind him when he had finished. He jumped slightly.

"I hope we didn't wake you," he said, looking pointedly in the direction of his children.

She patted his shoulder. "Not at all."

He'd never been able to bring up Lystra to his now-wife. He didn't know how exactly to state that he'd been in contact with a ghost without making it seem like he was insane.

He thought for a moment. "I'll be back. Hold down the fort while I'm gone?" He kissed her on the cheek, and walked over to the door to grab his keys and coat. "I shouldn't be longer than an hour."

Oliver got into his car and set off down the road.

It hadn't taken him long to find this place. A few well-directed searches had led him right there not long after Lystra's ascension.

The graveyard was peaceful, as it always was. He hadn't brought anything with him, so he picked a few blue wildflowers along the fence line and walked inside. It didn't take long for him to find the right headstone.

In loving memory of Lystra Flowers, with her date of birth and death written underneath. He once almost added the day she was finally, actually, laid to rest, but he didn't like the idea of defacing her headstone or being asked too many questions on the matter.

He laid the wildflowers down on the headstone. He kissed the tips of his fingers and pressed them against the cold, hard stone. He shut his eyes, and truly wished her well.

"You didn't know her as well as I did," a voice said from behind.

"Go away, Colton. You shouldn't be here."

Colton, hands shoved in his pockets, stepped forward and completely disregarded Oliver's request. "I have every right as you."

"You stole her song," Oliver said, glaring at the man. "You don't get to be here."

"I've come to peace with that," Colton said, pulling a hand from his pocket and taking out three stones. He laid them atop the headstone, with the largest in the middle and two smaller ones on either side. "Lystra taught me some very valuable lessons, and for that, I'm eternally grateful."

There was a long moment where neither man spoke. They simply existed in the same space and grew to understand each other. "What did she look like, as a ghost?" Oliver asked, at last breaking the silence. He'd always wanted to know.

Colton brought his eyes up to meet Oliver's. "Just as beautiful as the photos, only slightly translucent."

Oliver nodded, looking up at the cloudless sky and smiling. "She was everything."

IYSTRA'S SONG

VIOLA TEMPEST